I FOUND THE BOOGEYMAN UNDER MY BROTHER'S CRIB

I FOUND HORROR

BEN FARTHING

For Kemry.
I found you.

.

ALSO BY BEN FARTHING

1

I HEARD my little brother cry in his nursery. A stranger laughed in response.

I leapt out of bed without thinking.

Exhaustion made trusting my senses tricky. But if I'd really heard that vindictive laugh then I needed to get to my brother.

I pulled open my door, aware that I was sacrificing at least a few minutes of the precious sleep I was allowed.

Bennet cried again. He was almost two, and I'd spent so much time with him this summer break that I instantly recognized this was a cry of either fear or pain. At least, I thought I did. It was so hard to be sure of assumptions like this that I had to double-check before I acted on them. Otherwise, I'd end up with another lecture from Mom and Dad about Making Good Decisions.

The hallway was dark except for a sliver of light from a

nightlight in the hall bathroom. Mom and Dad's door was cracked. It was even darker in there.

I rushed to Bennet's room, between mine and my parents'. Through his cries, I listened to hear that stranger's laugh again. It had been male, raspy, and unkind. The sound of a bully closing in on prey.

Had I dreamed it?

It was hard to tell, lately.

I flipped Bennet's light switch, connected to an outlet which powered a floor lamp. The lamp didn't turn on.

"Bennet," I whispered.

His crying stopped. He only knew a few words, but he did have a unique way of saying my name, Rachel. I heard it now in response to my whisper, a desperate, begging little voice. "Tico!"

I moved through the dark toward my brother.

A heavy, grunting breath split the air between us. I froze.

"Dad?" I asked the dark space before me. "Are you in here?"

I couldn't imagine why Dad would be laughing so meanly at his little boy, but the fact that I couldn't imagine why didn't mean much. I wasn't living up to our family standards, and it was taking its toll on my mind.

On the other hand, he did occasionally sleepwalk.

Bennet's crib *thumped* as if the whole thing had lifted up and then struck the wood floor.

Bennet wailed.

"Dad?" I asked again. "Why aren't you picking him up? Are you awake?"

No answer.

My little brother again called for me. "Tico, up me!" He'd be raising his arms to be picked up, flexing his little fingers.

My heart broke for him. I stepped forward in the dark room. I reached up to turn on the ceiling light which Mom had installed when we moved in.

As my fingers found the metal chain, a gritty chuckle again came from next to Bennet's crib, directly in front of me.

I wasn't imagining it. Someone was in here with me, and it didn't sound like Dad.

I hesitated to pull the chain and click on the light. That's how deeply my parents had ingrained in me that between the hours of eleven and four, we slept, and we did not turn on the light.

But then someone exhaled onto my face. Warm, moist air splashing against my eyes to blossom down my cheeks and up my brow.

I jumped back. The overhead light's chain caught between my fingers as I tripped. The light flashed on for a brief moment before my hand slipped free.

In that light, where I'd thought Dad might be sleep-walking, I saw a mouth.

Gray, mottled lips over rotting but perfectly straight teeth. The edges of the mouth curled up into a stiff smile.

And around the mouth, as if they were outlining a clownish smile, were more teeth sticking through skin. Incisors pierced an upper lip. Molars stuck through cheeks. Bottom teeth stuck through the gray skin of a chin. Crusty blood circled each wound. Dried pus marked an infection.

This was all my eyes took in before the momentum of my fall made the chain slip from my fingers and the light snapped back off, returning the room to darkness.

2

MY BUTT HIT the wood floor beside the rug. My elbow hit the windowsill.

But adrenaline drowned out the pain.

The darkness was no longer empty.

That wasn't Dad between me and the crib. I didn't know who or what it was. I'd only been able to focus on one thing during that brief moment of light: a mouth circled by a ring of protruding teeth.

Bennet's crib thumped once again.

Either I screamed or Bennet finally cried loud enough to wake my parents, because their bedside lamps clicked on.

Coming from down the hall, the light was enough to bathe Bennet's room in grays and shadows.

No one was here.

But from my low vantage point on the floor, I could see into the darkness below the crib.

Where there should have been plastic tubs full of extra diapers, instead the space below the crib was empty. And through that space, I saw another room.

I looked above and to the sides of Bennet's crib. There was a window with curtains drawn, there were the prints of classic children's book covers that Dad had hung up. But when I looked underneath Bennet's crib, it was a low, rectangular tunnel into another child's dark room. The darkness blurred what could be seen, but I could make out a bookshelf, a rocking chair, and a crooked doorway that glowed with a faint, yellow light.

It made no sense. The only thing on the far side of this wall should be our front yard.

But I could see another room.

In my exhausted mind, I was sure that the thing with the mouth had gone under the crib, into that room, and out that glowing yellow door.

With sudden terror, I realized I hadn't seen Bennet since Mom and Dad had turned on their lights. Was he still in his crib? Or were his cries coming from the far side of this tunnel, from within that crooked bedroom which mirrored his own?

I scrambled across the floor toward the crib, stumbling to my feet, already imagining my little brother struggling in the arms of whoever owned such a terrible mouth.

Dad spoke behind me. "Rachel?" Perfectly awake and aware, despite being jolted out of sleep.

"Is he still here?" I blurted out as I crashed into the wood dowels of the crib.

Bennet was in the back corner of his crib, face pressed into the mattress, hugging a *Sesame Street* board book to his chest while he howled.

I scooped him up, feeling more relief than I'd thought could exist. He stiffened his arms and legs, not fighting me but also not relaxing at my touch.

Even in the dark room, I could see his face was beet red. "It's me," I cooed. "I'm here."

Over Bennet's screams, Dad asked, "What's going on? Did you wake him up?"

I became suddenly very aware that my ankles were right in front of the tunnel to that crooked room with its glowing yellow doorway. If the thing with the mouth came back, I was in reach.

I jumped away. "There was someone in here!" I said.

At that, I heard Mom's voice. "What?" Her footsteps pounded down the hallway to reach her little boy. She flipped the light switch. The floor lamp by the rocking chair turned on.

I flinched at the bright light.

That lamp hadn't turned on for me.

Although, my head felt so thick with exhaustion, I couldn't remember if I'd even tried the light switch.

Bennet saw Mom and reached for her. I handed him over. He wiped his nose on the shoulder of her pajamas, slowly getting control of his sobs.

I relaxed into that same safety that my little brother felt. Mom and Dad were here. We were okay now.

"What did you say?" Mom asked.

The sight of that mouth shot back into my mind. "I saw someone."

I dropped to my knees to look under the crib. Two plastic tubs. Behind those, drywall and wood trim.

No tunnel. No mysterious room on the other side. No crooked doorway with that eerie yellow glow.

Dad tugged at the windows, checking that they were locked. "What do you mean, *someone*?"

"I heard Bennet crying and someone laughing so I got up. I thought it was you but it was dark. I fell and the light flashed and I only saw his mouth."

Mom cradled Bennet against her chest while she checked the closet. Its accordion door squeaked as she pulled it open. "We would have seen anyone leaving down the hallway."

Dad slid the curtains back into place. "The windows are locked from the inside. Honey, why are you out of bed?"

"I told you," I started to say, but shame blossomed beneath my sternum and swelled until I felt my cheeks blush.

I'd messed up.

The tunnel and the crooked room and that mouth circled by teeth stabbing through skin—none of it could be real.

I tried to clear my head but I was just so tired. "I thought I heard someone. And I saw... I don't know."

Mom cooed to Bennet as she bounced him in her arms. My little brother was exhausted from being woken up a quarter after midnight. He was still too young to understand that sleep was how he would get rid of this feeling of exhaustion, and so he angrily ground his forehead into Mom's shoulder.

"Rachel," a bit of anger injected itself into Dad's otherwise caring tone. "This isn't okay. You can't wake up your brother like this and blame it on a nightmare."

I hadn't called it that.

But what was it?

My belly twisted with shame as my mind settled on the answer.

Mom sighed. She spoke quietly to Dad. "I'm going to get Bennet settled. Will you talk to her?"

Dad sighed. "Let's have some ice cream."

3

I FOLLOWED Dad to the kitchen. He motioned for me to sit at the table, and then he got out two spoons and a cardboard half-gallon of Rocky Road.

He handed me one spoon and sat across from me. "You know you can talk to me and your mom about anything, right?"

I knew that. "Yeah."

"So what's been going on? You've been abrasive lately."

I scooped a bite of ice cream into my mouth, giving myself time to also swallow the wave of guilt that swept over me. Despite my best efforts, I wasn't living how I should.

I couldn't answer his question. I realize now that he should have known the answer himself, but for as hard as they tried as parents, Mom and Dad had a big blind spot.

Before I tell you the rest of this story, I need you to understand why I was so tired, and why that made me feel like I was letting down my family. Why I lived my sixteenth year as a perpetual lump of shame.

You might have met someone who only needs four or five hours of sleep each night. Whatever magic your body does while it's asleep so you don't feel tired the next day, these people can do that magic twice as fast as the average person.

Both my mom and my dad are like that.

And they're both pretty bad at empathy. They're generally loving and supportive, but ask them to imagine a hardship they haven't personally been through, and they'll swear up and down that it could be solved with self-discipline and elbow grease.

So because Mom and Dad only need five hours of sleep to feel well rested, that's all I'm allowed to have. They recognized that growing children need more sleep, but the day I turned sixteen, Dad woke me up at four. That night, he made me stay up until eleven.

That first night I saw the thing that entered Bennet's room from under the crib, I'd been sixteen for seven months. Plenty long enough for exhaustion to seep deep into my brain.

And here's the thing: I respected the hell out of my parents. My inability to stay awake felt like a physical weakness, a moral failing, and a disappointment to my family name.

In hindsight, I was a confused young woman who wanted my parents' respect.

Which is why, as chocolate-covered almonds and slow-churned vanilla ice cream lit up my tastebuds, I felt more than fear about hallucinating a mouth with a ring of infected teeth and an impossible bedroom next to my little brother's. Because a hallucination meant that I wasn't sleeping enough. Except I knew—*I knew*—that productive adults only needed five hours each night. So that crooked room with its glowing yellow door was evidence that something was deeply wrong with me. If I couldn't live this simple schedule that my parents said was the reason for their success in life, then I was going to screw up this whole family.

Rocky Road ice cream did little to assuage my shame.

Dad snipered a ribbon of marshmallow fluff. "I'm worried about you, Rachel. You haven't had night terrors since you were ten. I can't remember you ever sleepwalking. But is that what happened tonight?"

"I guess so," I lied. I was fully awake, so it hadn't been a nightmare. The only explanation was delusion triggered by my weakness.

Dad put down his spoon. "What do you think's causing the bad dreams? Are you stressed about something?"

I didn't believe I should feel stressed. I told myself that this proper sleep schedule was difficult now, but once I got used to it my life would be so much happier than it would be otherwise.

My parents were doing this because it was good for me in the long run.

But right now I was in the thick of it, and I hated how difficult it was, and how weak that made me feel.

I didn't want to admit to that, so I lied again to my dad. "I'm stressed about going back to school."

"Ah." Dad smiled. "See, that's the sort of thing you need to talk about with your mom and me. You've got a few more weeks before your junior year starts. Let's plan a little vacation before then. I'll take off work."

"Okay," I said.

"For now, back to bed." Dad stood up to put away the ice cream, "Less than three hours until it's time to rise and shine. After this little adventure, we're all going to be sleepy tomorrow."

A few minutes later, I slipped back under my covers, where my warmth still lingered. My mattress and sheets were the best that money could buy. My blackout curtains banished the moonlight, keeping my sacred sleeping space in perfect darkness. My white noise machine played a fuzzy hum of what Mom called "brown noise," which drowned out the insects and chirper frogs in our yard. It was also supposed to let me sleep through Bennet's bad nights, but obviously that didn't always work.

Alone in my artfully designed sleeping environment, without the immediate need to make Mom and Dad proud, it was easy to slip back into the delusion of what I'd seen earlier. No sounds or sights to distract me. Only the memory of looking under the crib, into that crooked room, and seeing its glowing yellow doorway. The sudden terror of when I hadn't known whether Bennet's cries were coming from inside his crib or from under it. The hate emanating from the thing with the extra teeth that wanted my little brother.

But before my fear could work itself back up into actual belief, sleep overtook me.

4
_____

I BLINKED and Dad switched my light on.

"Time to wake up," Dad said. "Idle hands are unhappy hands."

My daily misery washed over me.

Dad flipped the light switch up and down. My bedside lamp flashed. "Up and at 'em."

That sort of thing was funny that first week of my new sleep rules. I was exhausted then, but I thought I was still adapting like Mom and Dad said I would. Twenty-one days to build a habit.

It wasn't funny any more, not that I would admit it.

Waking up was the worst part of the day—those first few minutes when I'd have to get out of bed or Dad would rip the covers off. My body was crying for more sleep, my head was heavy with exhaustion, and all I could think about was how long until 11?

And I knew it was impacting my mood. I tried so hard to push aside the snippiness, the short temper at Bennet's cries, the general unhappiness that accompanied my exhaustion.

Mom and Dad called it hormones.

I really, really wanted to believe them.

"It's Mom's turn to make breakfast," Dad said, waiting in the doorway for me to get out of bed.

I threw my legs over the edge.

I felt worse this morning than normal. I tried to remember why.

"Pancakes with chocolate chips," Dad said. "Do you want to go for a jog? If not, could you stay here and listen for Bennet in case he wakes up early?"

"I'll stay," I yawned. My head felt even heavier than normal. "I need a second to wake up."

Dad *hmmed*. "I thought you might. Do you remember having a nightmare? You woke us all up."

Everything from the night before came flooding back into the front of my mind.

Bennet's cry, the male voice in there with him, the brief glimpse of that thing's mouth and then the other room that connected to Bennet's beneath his crib.

It's crazy to think I could have forgotten those sights my mind conjured up, but it's hard to convey how difficult it was to think straight when I'd been sleep deprived for half the year.

"Sorry. I won't do it again." I saw on Dad's face that he believed me. That kept my shame from growing. But it stayed there and it bubbled. If I weren't so weak, then this sleep schedule wouldn't have made me hallucinate.

How long until I got used to this? How long was it going to hurt until I got to the part about "good for me in the long run?"

"Please don't beat yourself up," Dad said. "People have nightmares sometimes. I still sleepwalk once in a while. It's okay. Let's not have it become a habit, though. Remember the value of healthy sleep."

"Right," I said.

"Breakfast in five." He left me alone in my room, lit only by my lamp.

I stumbled to my closet. My mind was a jumble of guilt and fear.

I reached for my closet's doorknob.

Metal clinked inside, the sound of empty coat hangers bumping into each other.

Ice ran down my spine.

If I opened the door, what would I find on the other side? Another entrance to that crooked room?

I saw myself opening my closet to confront a shadowy figure with only its mouth visible, teeth straight and smiling and rotten green, with a ring of extra teeth circling the mouth, stabbing out from infected skin.

My head was so heavy it pulled me forward; how could I do anything except follow it inside my closet?

A frying pan crashed in the kitchen, the noise echoing down the hall.

I snapped fully awake, still standing in front of my closed closet door.

Telling myself it was all a delusion, I didn't stick around to hear the tinkling clothes hangers again.

I left my room and headed to breakfast in my pajamas.

I could get dressed after the sun came up.

5
***

THE SUN ROSE, starting the path across the sky that in fourteen hours would send it back down below the horizon. I tried not to think that far ahead, worried about what my brain might conjure up in another night of darkness.

But I had all day.

After breakfast, Bennet woke up happy. He babbled a drawn out rendition of the theme from *Reading Rainbow*, which Mom was proud to say was his favorite show. He couldn't have understood much of it, but something about LeVar hypnotized him.

I'd been reading on the couch, but had moved to the wood floor so I wouldn't nod off, when Bennet's song drifted down the hallway. "Eeeee aayyyyy oooooooh."

Dad had left for work and Mom was showering before taking Bennet to daycare and then heading to her own job, so it fell on me to get him up.

I didn't want to go in his room. It scared me, the idea of

confronting what had been in there last night. Simultaneously, weighty shame fell on my shoulders, telling me that my hallucinations proved I was too weak to be a good member of this family.

Exhaustion allowed me to fear that room as if what I'd seen were real at the same time that I felt guilty for hallucinating it.

But exhaustion also removed any and all time between impulse and action, so the moment that Bennet's happy song shifted toward impatience, I ran down the hall, swept him out of his crib, and danced back out, grabbing a clean diaper and clothes on the way.

While Mom finished getting ready, I got Bennet into a pair of lime green shorts and a t-shirt with a slogan about believing in yourself. I fed him half his breakfast at the table, and the other half I hand-fed to him while I followed him around the living room.

Mom came in a few minutes later, dressed in khakis and a blouse, ready to tackle a workday's worth of our county's legal problems.

Bennet and I were using board books to build a little house.

"Thank you so much for getting him ready. Now I've got a few minutes to sit down with you guys before I have to go."

She sat cross-legged and we all three built a little neighborhood out of Dr. Seuss, Sandra Boyton, and Margaret Wise Brown.

After a minute, Mom said, "When I used to wake up

from nightmares, I liked to count all the different things I could feel. Like my warm sheets, my soft pajamas on my skin, the air in my nostrils as I breathed. That's how I convinced myself that I wasn't dreaming anymore and I was safe now. It's also good mindfulness practice for your whole life, to keep yourself centered."

"Thanks."

Bennet fussed as *Goodnight Moon* refused to be a roof. Mom fixed it, and we built out the book town.

"Time for us to head out." Mom scooped up Bennet. "Are you sticking with your schedule today?"

Mom and Dad didn't dictate my time during the summer, but they did require that *I* dictated my time. Each June they sat down with me as I wrote out five different daily schedules filled with success-building activities like reading, going for walks, watching documentaries, and calling elderly relatives to chat and help their loneliness. (Loneliness was a negative experience Mom and Dad could empathize with, since they said they were both lonely before they met each other.)

"Yeah, I've got my schedule picked out," I said.

"Good." She kissed me on the forehead and brought me into a hug that included Bennet. He wrapped his arm around my neck and exaggerated a kissing noise.

Mom said, "Call if you need anything. I'll have my phone on me all day."

They left.

I found myself alone in our empty house.

The living room and kitchen were open to each other,

and then a narrow hallway led to my room, Bennet's room, and then our parents'.

I was still in my pajamas. Sunlight now came through the front window, lighting up a beam of floating dust on its way to spotlight the abandoned board book neighborhood that we'd made.

I could go get dressed.

I just had to go down the narrow hallway, into my room, and then open the closet.

Instead, I put on my flip-flops and went outside to bring the trashcan back from the road.

Already at eight in the morning, the summer heat was uncomfortable. Although, not as bad as the humidity where we used to live.

Sunlight on my skin in the mornings felt so *wrong* ever since my new life of so little sleep. At any given moment, my body was so tired that it was convinced it must be nighttime, so the sun always felt like it was rising too early.

I walked slowly to the end of the driveway, giving myself more time outside, away from my closet and Bennet's room.

My neighbor's front door creaked open.

Landon came outside to get his own trash can. He was a year older than me, going into his senior year. He had a snorting laugh and a tendency to talk too long about Trivial Pursuit sessions with his mom. But in the summer he was the only person my age on our street, and so we'd become decent friends. We hung out some days and had a text chain going about the cartoon *Avatar*, which he'd convinced me to watch.

"Hey, Rachel." Landon noted my pajamas. "You didn't just wake up, did you?"

Landon knew about my parents' rules. I'd taken a single nap while hanging out with him, before the guilt ate me up too much. Plus, Landon didn't hide very well that my disobedience bothered him, even if he thought the sleep schedule was strange.

"No, we got up at the normal time."

"You look more tired than usual." Landon's eyes suddenly widen. "I'm sorry, you're not supposed to say that to girls."

"It's okay. Our night got interrupted." Why did I say that? I didn't want to go back over the events that both scared and embarrassed me.

The truth was, I needed to talk to someone about it, and Landon was nice.

His eyebrows furrowed with genuine concern. "Bennet didn't wander off again, did he?"

A week earlier, I'd left the front door cracked after getting the mail. Bennet had wiggled his little fingers in the crack to open it. He didn't "wander off" so much as go to the mailbox himself, mimicking what he saw me do each day. When he couldn't reach it, he tried climbing the mailbox, fell, and started crying. That's how Landon found him. Our street isn't busy, but it was a scary thing to happen. Mom and Dad were mad at me for leaving the door open, but my guilt over the incident was already at max level.

"No," I told Landon now. "We're all fine."

"Here, let me get your trash can." Landon hurried over to my driveway. He leaned the trashcan back on its wheels.

I didn't need his chivalry or his strength—the can was empty, after all—but the walk back to the side of the house would be a natural time to spew my heart out.

"I'm still getting used to my parents' sleep schedule," I said.

"That'd be a tough one. I'm glad my mom has different rules."

"I woke up last night and thought I heard someone in Bennet's room." My damned impulsiveness. Ever since I turned 16, sometimes the words came out before I even realized they were in my head.

Landon stopped walking. "Who was in there? Your parents?"

"No. A man with a mean laugh. But he wasn't really there. I was just so tired I've started seeing things."

"You mean hearing things."

"No, I went in there and I saw him."

"You did? Who was it?"

"The light was only on him for a second. All I saw was his mouth. It was gross."

"Wow, Rachel. What happened? Did you call the police?"

"No, that's what I'm saying. When my parents came in Bennet's room there was nobody in there. It was all in my head. I'm trying so hard to get used to only sleeping five hours, but it's only getting worse. Now I'm seeing things."

Landon went quiet. He started pulling the trashcan again, its wheels rumbling on the pavement.

I'd only seen him like this once before, when his mom had made him knock on our door to ask Dad to stop mowing their side of the grass between our driveways.

He had something on his mind that he didn't want to say.

"What is it?" I prodded.

"How long have you guys lived here now? Like four years?"

"Three," I said. "Why?"

"You know there was a house here before yours, right?"

"Wasn't that forever ago?"

"It burned down when I was a kid. It was the old farmhouse from before this was a neighborhood. Big upstairs, basement."

"We don't have a basement, not even a crawlspace. The house is on a cement slab. Dad's always upset he has to run a dehumidifier."

Landon talked over me to keep me on topic. "They filled the basement after the old house burnt down. The point is, my second cousins lived there. That's why my mom moved us here after my dad... well, that part's not important. My second cousin told me about seeing a man in the house. My mom and her family would tell stories about the Boogeyman to keep us in line, so that's what my cousin called it."

I didn't want to entertain what he was suggesting. "You're telling me this because…"

"You saw someone, didn't you?"

A mouth with an extra ring of teeth protruding through inflamed skin.

"It's this schedule my parents have me on. I'm not adjusted yet and my body and brain are doing weird things. I didn't see anybody. My parents would have seen them getting away." Unless they fled under the crib, to that crooked bedroom with the glowing yellow doorway.

"My mom could probably tell you more stories, if you wanted. She saw the Boogeyman herself, as a kid. It was at her cousins house, too."

A rare rational thought pushed its way through the mess that was my brain. "Hold on, are you really suggesting I saw the Boogeyman?"

Landon studied my face for an intense, brief moment. "I'm just saying what my family has seen around here."

"But the Boogeyman?" I felt myself making a bigger deal of this than it was. I could blame my exhaustion-related lack of impulse control, but it was also nice to mock the idea, make it smaller. "The thing under your bed? The monster in your closet?"

My throat caught and my ears rang with the sound of clothes hangers *tinking* against each other.

"What?" Landon asked. "You just thought of something."

"Nothing. Thanks for your help with the trash can."

Alone in the house would be better than out here with Landon's stories.

"I think you should be careful, is all."

"Yeah, I'll be on the lookout for any creeps." I looked him in the eye on the last word.

I left Landon and the trash can in the middle of the driveway. I went inside to tackle the activities on my schedule that I could do without going near the bedrooms.

6

FOUR HOURS BEFORE SUNSET, Dad got home with Bennet. He and Mom staggered their work days by two hours so they could spend more time with us.

He suggested we do some mindfulness yoga to help me relax and hopefully avoid nightmares. It was tricky with Bennet crawling over us, but it was nice.

Landon texted me. *Sorry for being weird this morning.*

I told him it was fine and shifted the conversation toward season two of *Avatar*. Landon asked for me to wait to watch the season finale with him. It was his birthday in two days, so I figured why not. His mom didn't do much to celebrate. The least I could do was watch a cartoon with him.

Dad made dinner, Mom got home, we ate, and Bennet went to bed.

The sun went down and I had two more hours until I was allowed to go to sleep.

I believe I sat on the couch and read for an hour. It's hard to remember what happened those days of so little sleep, apart from the incidents that really stand out.

We all had our individual "winding down routine," and usually Mom and Dad's involved going in their room and shutting the door at ten.

My routine was to very slowly get ready for bed, closing my eyes for as much of it as possible. It began with a long, warm shower. Dad suggested that morning showers be cold in order to wake you up, so I bathed at night.

That night, when I flipped the bathroom light switch, one of the three bulbs above the mirror popped and went out.

The shadows that normally lived behind the toilet and beneath the window curtain now spread further up the walls.

I tried to pretend everything was normal, keeping my eyes closed while getting the shower ready. The less light that made it into my eyes, the deeper I would sleep once the clock hit eleven. At least, that's what I told myself.

I got in the shower. The hiss of the shower head and the warmth of the water were nearly as relaxing as sleep.

I closed my eyes as I lathered lavender shampoo into my hair.

Sometimes I thought I could drift off while washing my hair in the warm shower.

A sour smell blended with the lavender. Almost like watermelon, but if it'd been candied and something went wrong.

The bathroom floor creaked.

I had too much soap dripping down my face to open my eyes. "Mom?"

No answer.

I frantically rinsed my hair.

The acrid smell grew stronger, thicker, like I was breathing in thick smog from a cartoon. I wanted to gag.

The floor creaked again, sounding farther down than it should with someone stepping on it, as if the sound were coming from within the floor.

I rubbed soapy water from my eyes.

I told myself that no one was there, that Dad might have snuck into the bathroom to grab something from the drawers, that the wind was making the house settle. It didn't matter if it made sense, I just needed an explanation that wasn't that thing (*Boogeyman*, Landon said) waiting to drag my little brother into that other room and through that glowing yellow doorway.

I knew as soon as I opened my eyes, I would see that mouth with those rotten, protruding teeth, inches from my face.

I got the soap away and opened my eyes.

Only the white linoleum of the shower, splattered with foamy bubbles from my frantic wiping.

That too-sweet melon smell still hung thick around me.

I turned my attention to the curtain, listening intently for any further creaks from the other side. Slowly, I pulled it open. The curtain rings made a metallic scraping noise, not unlike the tinkling of metal hangers.

I peeked around the curtain. Fog covered the mirror and left condensation on the sink and toilet. No one was in here.

I exhaled.

It was all in my head. Embarrassing, but in that moment I was happy to be delusional rather than have the Boogeyman in the bathroom with me.

The sweet smell was fading, but still distinct. Still so different from the mild flowering scent of my lavender shampoo.

I noticed a new hand soap dispenser on the counter. Mom must have bought a new scent. Why she'd pick *too-sweet watermelon*, I had no idea.

Nothing strange going on. I was only exhausted and freaked out.

I finished washing, dried off, and then put on my pajamas. Before I left the bathroom, I sniffed the new hand soap.

Lavender, like my shampoo.

7

I SWITCHED off the bathroom light, leaving the hallway in darkness.

That familiar strip of light from beneath Mom and Dad's door wasn't enough to guide my way to my room. Not after I'd been in the bright bathroom.

I dashed for my bedroom and switched on my lamp. My room was normal. I closed my eyes, listening.

I heard my parents' murmuring conversation. But the creaking from the bathroom floor had stopped.

My heart raced. I was too freaked out.

How long would these delusions last, and how long would I be afraid of the dark?

The clock said I had another thirty minutes before I could turn out my light and go to sleep.

None of the activities on my various evening schedules sounded like they could both keep me awake and stop me from dwelling on the scary things I'd seen.

The things I *thought* I'd seen.

It was harder to believe I was delusional, this late at night.

I suddenly wanted to check on Bennet.

Leaving my door open to let the light into the hallway, I slipped over into his room.

Even over the white noise machine, I heard his little snoring.

I stepped lightly, approaching his crib so I could see him.

Bennet lay on his back, one arm sprawled out, the other cradling a board book against his side. His *Hungry, Hungry Caterpillar* blanket was up to his belly.

I scanned the room.

No Boogeyman standing near his crib, or sitting in the rocking chair, or hiding in the open closet.

That left one place to check.

I crouched down to look under the crib.

Only the plastic tubs that should be there.

I sighed, whether from relief or fear, I don't know.

Then I went back to my room and sat up straight on the edge of my bed, waiting for bedtime to arrive. If I started to drift off, I only had to hear my parents move about in their room, and the fear of being caught snapped me back awake.

Finally, my parents' lamp clicked off. The strip of light beneath their door disappeared.

I stood up, turned on my phone light, switched off my light switch, and then got into bed.

Once I was safely under the covers, I turned off my phone.

This was the only part of the day when I was completely relaxed. And every night, it seemed to last less and less time.

I fell asleep in seconds.

I woke to Bennet fussing.

Darkness still filled the house.

My room smelled like too-sweet watermelon, so much so that I wondered if that's what actually woke me up. Because Bennet's fussing hadn't advanced to screaming yet.

I wanted to go check on him. Or what I really wanted was to hear Mom and Dad go check on him.

I didn't want to get out of bed. My covers were a shield against what might hide in the dark.

Shame roiled in my gut. If I was afraid, how much more afraid would my toddler brother be?

I sat up, ready to go check on Bennet.

I heard the *thump* of Dad's feet hitting the floor. Footsteps from down the hallway. Bennet's fussing paused as Dad either picked him up or found his pacifier.

Before I could plummet back to sleep, the stench of overly sweet watermelon bloomed into an overwhelming, invisible, noxious gas.

I gagged at the scent.

What was this?

Since Dad was already up, I'd go ask him if he knew what was going on with the smell.

I fumbled on my nightstand for my phone, found it, and turned on the flashlight.

I expected to see some evidence of what this smell was coming from, but all I saw was my room and the strange shadows made by my furniture.

I avoided looking at my closed closet door.

I hurried out of bed and flipped my light switch, adding a bit more light to the hallway.

Bennet's fussing advanced to wailing.

Stupid of me to not realize my light would bother him while Dad was trying to get him back to sleep. I turned it back off.

Dad hummed to Bennet in his baritone, a melody I didn't recognize.

Another *thump* like Dad had bumped into the crib.

I walked out into the hallway to ask about the smell. I kept my light pointed straight down at the floor to avoid bothering Bennet.

At the end of the hallway, Mom and Dad's door opened. Dad appeared, groggy, putting on his bathrobe.

He saw me. "What are you doing up?"

My heart dropped to my gut.

I whipped my phone light up to point into Bennet's room.

I saw—and there was no longer any doubt that what I was seeing was real—a bulky man in a tattered yellow raincoat stained with something dark and something grass green. Its arms were both too long and too fat. Its elbows were down by its waist. The sleeves of the yellow raincoat were ripped where flannel elbows beneath had burst through. There was no muscular shape to the bulk, but instead it reminded me of boa constrictors that I'd seen on our educational trip to the zoo.

It hunched over Bennet's crib. Its hands were too small for its arms, but from those disturbingly normal hands my little brother dangled by his armpits.

As my light shined on this thing that couldn't be a man, it turned to face me.

This time I saw more than that mouth, with its stiff, rotten smile, and its extra teeth piercing through the skin of its cheeks, its upper lips, its chin—I saw its eyes, gray skin surrounding eyes that could be human if they didn't look so faded, as if they'd seen too much of time and were slipping away from existence, and before long there'd be no eyes at all, only blank, gray flesh.

These eyes looked through me, likely not seeing past the gleam of my light, but they stared with icy hate.

With my light, Bennet finally saw who was holding him. He screamed and twisted his torso.

All this I saw in a heartbeat.

My protectiveness collided with my exhaustion-induced impulsiveness—I let out a big sister's war cry and charged the Boogeyman.

"Rachel?" Dad spoke incredulously from his open doorway.

My hand clipped the doorframe. My phone dropped to the floor, flashlight pointed down.

The room went black.

I collided with the crib. The intruder had moved out of my path. Bennet's cries came from in front of me, so I reached down and scooped him up.

He must have twisted free from the intruder.

I slammed into the crib a second time, even as I stood still. The same thing had happened last night.

The crib itself had risen to strike me. That was the *thump* I'd heard. The intruder escaping back under the crib, to that crooked and blurry room, where it could disappear through that glowing yellow doorway.

Dad flipped on the light switch. Bennet's lamp turned on. "What in the world are you doing?"

"He was in here!" I declared, now sure that I wasn't crazy, that I wasn't so weak that this family was making me delusional.

"Oh, not again," Dad said quietly.

I pushed my crying brother into Dad's arms, then dropped to my hands and knees to look under the crib. "It went under here."

Except there was nothing out of place. "No," I said to myself.

"There's no one in here," Dad said. "You had a nightmare again."

But this time I knew I wasn't dreaming and I wasn't delusional. I didn't sleepwalk in here and make a scene that made Bennet cry. Dad was standing in the hallway, already awake, by the time I did anything.

My little brother had almost been taken by that thing —by the Boogeyman.

"It was real," I said. "And it's after Bennet."

Mom appeared in the doorway. "No more of this," she ordered. "Rachel, to the kitchen. We're going to have a talk."

First I needed to be absolutely sure that Bennet was safe. I pulled the plastic totes out from under the crib. Nothing else under there but hardwood floor and the wall. I checked the locks on the windows as if that mattered.

"Rachel," Mom said, "now."

I held her gaze a second longer than was respectful. "Don't leave Bennet by himself." I confidently strode to the kitchen, buzzed on exhaustion, adrenaline, and fear.

As I passed my room, I noticed the acrid watermelon smell still lingered. Had I noticed it in Bennet's room?

8

Mom and I sat across from each other at the kitchen table.

She didn't get out the ice cream.

"Dad's staying with Bennet, right?"

"Don't worry about that right now. We're talking about you."

I could have kept up my defiance against Mom's anger. But she let disappointment slip into her tone. It deflated me.

I tried to speak with confidence, but I heard myself whine, "You need to call the police."

"Not for a nightmare."

I swallowed. Gathered the words and how I would deliver them. "It was real."

My self-esteem bounced harmlessly off Mom's distant demeanor. "There's no one in our house but us."

"I know what I saw."

Mom sighed. "I'm worried about you."

My gut knotted. She was about to offer me something else to be ashamed of. My eyes burned. I did *not* want to cry in front of Mom right now.

"These sort of delusions can happen when you're not sleeping enough."

I would have argued again about the Boogeyman being a delusion, but the fact that Mom was considering that our family sleep schedule might be wrong for me was too much to ignore. Was there finally a light at the end of this tunnel?

"I've read that, too," I said cautiously.

"Are you sleeping enough?"

Her directness stunned me. I'd been afraid to bring this up, afraid that asking for leeway would mean letting them down. "No," I whispered, grateful for this sudden compassion.

But Mom's answer was full of venom. She slapped the table. "I knew it. Your father said I was assuming too much, but I knew it."

I shrank into my chair. "What?"

"How long have you been sneaking out of bed at night?"

Tears formed in my eyes. I didn't want to feel like a child and so I scoffed at Mom. I heard how derisive it sounded.

"Watch your tone, young lady. We've taught you to value your sleep. Our bodies need five hours each night, and that's the rule we've set in this house. Have you been skipping out on sleep since you turned sixteen? Or even before that?"

I could hardly form the words, her accusation shocked me so much. "I sleep every second I'm allowed."

"If that were the case, you wouldn't be hallucinating someone in Bennet's room."

I stood up too quickly and knocked over my chair. "I'm not sitting here for this. I'm too tired and I'm too scared for Bennet." On saying his name I had to choke down a sob.

"Fine," Mom said. "Go to bed and pretend to sleep. But stay out of your brother's room. He needs his rest just as much as you."

I started back to my room, wiping my eyes. I stopped at the entrance to the hallway. Bennet's room was once again dark and Mom and Dad's bedroom door was closed. Dad had already quieted Bennet and gone back to bed.

Two nights in a row now, this intruder had come for my little brother. Would it come a second time in one night?

I stood at the end of the hallway, while Mom switched off the kitchen light and walked up to me.

"Go on," she said. "We both need to get back to bed."

"I thought Dad was staying with Bennet."

"It's two in the morning. Everyone's going back to sleep."

"It's not safe."

"We're not going through this again. Back to bed. And give me your phone. No staying up late to play on the internet."

"I can't. It's my only flashlight."

"You don't need a flashlight, you're going to sleep. Give it to me, now."

You'll need to have patience with me. I was still a kid and I had no identity outside of my parents approval. It wasn't until much later in my life that I learned to ignore that tone that said, "*If you're a good person, you'll do what I say.*"

And so that night, I gave Mom my only flashlight and went to my room.

But I knew I wasn't delusional, and so once she went back to bed, I sat by my open door, listening intently for any movement from Bennet's room.

It was going to be a long, dark night.

9

SITTING VULNERABLE ON MY FLOOR, my cold toes and my fear helped keep me awake.

That scent had faded, but I kept catching hints of it. It was connected to the Boogeyman—he must have been in my room before going after Bennet.

I hugged myself over my oversized t-shirt, one of Dad's that had worn down to comfy softness. It was too thin for sitting on this cold floor in the middle of the night.

They say that darkness strengthens your other senses, but really it confuses them. Hard to tell where sounds are coming from or exactly what they are.

I'd lately been so quick to fall asleep that I wasn't used to being alone with the noises of our house at night.

The chilly air conditioning blew out of a vent in the ceiling. A sharp tapping in the walls, which ages ago Dad had explained to me was the water pressure adjusting as night cooled the pipes.

A memory came to me, sitting like this with my knees against my chest, except on my parents' floor in the middle of the night. I'd had a nightmare, and I knew if I crawled into bed with them, they'd carry me back to my own room. And so I made myself comfortable sitting on the floor. Even asleep, their presence helped me feel safe.

In my dark room now, I could imagine that I was once again younger than sixteen, before Mom and Dad's compassion was overshadowed by this new family rule, before I lived every moment with the knowledge that I was holding my family back.

I closed my eyes.

I was a kid again. My head on my knees was like laying on my Dad's chest. The susurration of the AC from my ceiling was like Dad's slow breathing. The taps from the pipes were Dad's fingernails on the wooden arms of his favorite chair, tapping the melodies of 80s country songs.

The arrhythmic creaks from under the bed were...

I opened my eyes to unyielding dark.

Something was under my bed.

It creaked like slow, careful footsteps, but in the dark the sound was too far below my bed, as if someone were walking through a pit in my floor.

I'd seen the crooked room through the tunnel beneath Bennet's crib. I could imagine a similar space under my own bed, a pit that stretched deeper than it was wide.

A chill went down my neck. It was one thing to act impulsively brave to protect my little brother. It was another thing to be sitting on my floor in my dark room, totally exposed.

Fear tingled through my body.

I wanted the safety of my covers.

Another creeping footstep, deep beneath my bed.

If I called for my parents, they wouldn't believe me. If I fled my bedroom, I'd be even more exposed—and Mom and Dad might catch me and that'd be proof I was skipping out on sleep.

I wanted back in bed.

I pictured myself trying to sneak back to my bedside, and then the thing in the pit reaching up to grab my ankles and yank me away.

My parents would think I'd run away after being scolded, and it'd be my fault when they felt guilty for the rest of their lives.

Worse, without me, Bennet would have no one to protect him.

Another slow creak. Closer to me this time.

I carefully got my feet underneath me. I stayed there, crouching.

The next creak sounded right below me, the pit was widening, it was inches from swallowing me up.

I jumped with as much strength as I could, soaring over the hole I knew had replaced my floor.

For a moment I was terrified that my bed would be gone, that I'd fall past it to the floor, but the floor would be gone and I'd fall into the gaping jaws of the Boogeyman, to be chewed up by rings of rotting teeth.

Then I landed on my mattress.

I scuttled to my headboard and pulled my covers up to my shoulders.

The creaking stopped.

I sat and waited.

No smells.

No noises.

Even sitting up, it was harder to stay awake in my bed than on the floor.

My eyelids grew heavy.

I blinked and my alarm went off.

4:00 a.m.

I raced on light feet to Bennet's room. My heart raced from fear of finding an empty crib.

He was sleeping peacefully under his blanket.

I hurried back as quietly as possible, barely making it to my room before Mom and Dad's door opened.

I switched on my light myself, to prove to them that I wasn't purposely avoiding sleep, and I was capable of getting up on time.

As I got dressed, I realized that I needed to talk to Landon again.

By tonight, the Boogeyman would come back for Bennet and my parents weren't going to do a thing about it. This time, I needed to be ready.

10

After Mom and Dad left for work and to take Bennet to daycare, I went over to find Landon.

I checked around his house to see if he was outside. After not finding him, I texted him.

I'm outside. Can we talk?

He opened his front door and looked uncomfortable to see me. Maybe our plans for watching cartoons on his birthday tomorrow hadn't smoothed over my rudeness in the driveway yesterday. He checked over his shoulder and then stepped outside to shut the door behind him.

"Did it happen again?" he asked.

I nodded. "I saw it this time. The Boogeyman. You're not crazy. I'm sorry." I felt silly saying its name out loud, but that's what it was.

Landon scratched at his cheek. "Are you sure? What did you see?"

I described how it looked in its tattered yellow raincoat, thick stiff arms but simple human hands, gray, rotting skin on its face, eyes that looked blurry like they were fading away, and that disturbing ring of scant teeth that pierced through the skin around its mouth.

Landon slowly exhaled.

I was too anxious now. I kept talking. "That's the Boogeyman you were talking about, right? The thing your cousin saw in the old house? The thing your mom saw when she was a kid."

"Sounds like it."

"So tell me what to do."

His head jerked backward on his skinny neck. "What do you mean?"

"How do I protect my brother?"

"From what?"

I knew I was exhausted, but I was still pretty sure that was a stupid question. "How do I keep my brother safe from the Boogeyman?"

"You can't. Or... I mean, you don't."

"I can't keep Bennet safe? How are you saying that so calmly?"

"He is safe."

"He absolutely is not. That thing picked him up. It wants to drag him under the crib."

Landon looked surprised. "What's under there?"

"That's where it comes from. I saw another room, all blurry and weird. I think that's where it comes from."

Landon seemed to pick his words carefully. "I've never heard of something like that."

"You said your mom knows more about this than you, right? Is she awake?"

He awkwardly rocked on his heels. I knew Mrs. Foster was a shy woman, but I needed help.

"I don't know. She's still mad about your dad cutting part of our grass."

"Please. I don't know what else to do."

Landon exhaled. "Wait here."

He went inside, leaving me in the morning sunshine.

Too much time passed. I knocked.

Landon opened the door. "I said to wait. Now Mom's gonna think you're rude for not being patient."

He waved me inside. The front door opened right into the living room.

Their house was darker than mine. Trees in their front yard diminished the morning sun. Smaller windows with thick curtains added extra protection against natural light.

A couch with worn out blue fabric sat against one wall, while a faded brown loveseat sat against another. Each was paired with a wicker basket full of magazines that looked older than me.

An older model Playstation was set up next to a small flat-screen TV, which was playing a historical documentary.

Mrs. Foster was sitting in a rocking chair by a bricked-up fireplace. She had an embroidery hoop in her lap, a design of a cabin by a river. Its stitching remained half-finished.

Landon's mom was much older than my parents. He'd been a surprise baby, as late as his mom could get pregnant. I knew she was retired, though from what sort of career I wasn't sure.

She looked up at me, wrinkled cheeks pulled taut by pursed lips. She paused the TV.

"Rachel. It's good to see you."

"Thank you. You, too." I could be the sort of polite that she wanted.

"I want to tell you that I admire you for enduring this hardship your parents are putting you through."

I felt some defensiveness at her suggesting that Mom and Dad were purposely making me suffer. Even more so, it sounded like a compliment and so I minimized my own effort. "It's not so bad. I stole naps here and there when I was still getting used to it. Even on your patio one time."

Mrs. Foster stiffened in her chair. "Landon was aware of this?"

I'd put my foot in my mouth.

Landon coughed. "I discouraged it."

That wasn't true.

What little inflection Mrs. Foster had in her voice went dry. "You are not to help anyone to disobey their parents."

"Yes ma'am," Landon said.

I tried to move us ahead in the conversation. "Landon said you could tell me about the Boogeyman."

Mrs. Foster gave her son one last stern look and then

turned her attention back to me. She tapped the TV remote on the edge of her embroidery hoop. "Why do you want to know about him?"

I looked at Landon. "Did you tell her yet?"

His mom raised a finger. "No. I want to hear it from you."

This should have been an awkward conversation, admitting that I believed I'd seen a monster from under the bed. But again, my exhaustion left my impulsivity unbridled. "A monster came into my little brother's room the last two nights. Landon said your sister lived in the old house that ours replaced and your family saw the Boogeyman there."

"Part of that is true," she said. "If this is the Boogeyman you've seen, and not a nightmare caused by your parents' sleep torture, then you need to know *why* it's come to your brother's room."

"They're not torturing me," I said.

Mrs. Foster glared at me while she spoke to her son. "Tell your friend not to argue with her elders, or you'll be grounded from TV."

"Please don't argue with Mom," Landon whispered. He looked proud.

Taken aback by their bizarre awkwardness, I kept my mouth shut.

Mrs. Foster settled into her chair. She put the TV remote on an end table and resumed her embroidery while she spoke. "Every culture has a story about the Boogeyman. In some, that story branched off from myths about the fae. The name Boogeyman, in some English-speaking places, comes from *boggart*, which is a wicked trickster fairy that causes chaos in people's homes. The Boogeyman may have once been a boggart, or he may have sprung off from them in whatever way fairies reproduce."

Now she was talking about fairies like they were real. That was crazy, but so was seeing the Boogeyman lift your brother from his crib. I kept listening.

"The Boogeyman isn't a trickster for the whole household. In the stories parents used to tell, he only has eyes for the children. If they go out at night, or if they're not careful in dark places, then the Boogeyman will get them."

I thought of Bennet wandering up to the mailbox. I was glad I hadn't left the door open after dark.

"These stories come from all over the world. The *Cucuy* in Mexico, the *Butzemann* in Germany, the *Bhoot* in India, or the *Ong ke* in Vietnam. They're all the same creature."

"The same type of creature or the exact same one?"

Mrs. Foster closed her eyes and shook her head, like she was shaking off my interruption. "Listen first, then ask questions."

"Clear your throat," Landon whispered. "If she pauses, then you can talk. That's how it'll work when we're older, so we have to learn it now."

I couldn't get over the *strangeness* of his respect for his mother. Why was I seeking help from these people? Their weird household dynamic almost seemed worse than my own problems. Almost.

Mrs. Foster continued. "In some of these cultures, the boogeyman gets more creative than making off with disobedient children. He might change his face to look like someone you know, or walk straight through a wall without leaving a mark."

I thought of the tunnel underneath Bennet's crib.

"But there's one thing all Boogeyman legends have in common: they're told to children."

"To scare them," Landon added.

"Correct," said his mom, apparently okay with interruptions if they matched the rhythm of her storytelling. "And here's where we need to remember one key fact about moms and dads: they tell stories in order to protect their children. And the Boogeyman comes from a story."

She paused enough that I felt comfortable clearing my throat and then saying, "I saw it. It wasn't in a story—it was in my house."

Mrs. Foster smiled triumphantly. I'd fallen for her wordplay. "I believe I said he *came* from a story, not that he's still in one. There's power in a parent's love, and just as much power in a parent's fear. So many parents, for so many centuries, all around the world, warning their children to stay in bed or the Boogeyman will get them. Eventually, all those warnings turn into something real."

I wanted to ask if it was a transformed fairy or a imaginary monster made real, but instead I asked, "You've seen it too, then?"

She shook her head, sadly. "No. My cousin did, but I've only heard him. Once, rustling the rug under Landon's bed. When I went to check, I heard the coat hangers rattle in the closet."

"I've heard that. And he has a smell, like watermelon injected with too much sugar."

Mrs. Foster's eyes widened. "I've smelled that before. I never made the connection. But then, I haven't seen him so clearly like you have."

"What about when your cousin saw it?" I asked.

"Her name is Sarah." She sighed, enjoying a fond memory. "She's quite a bit older than me, not unlike the age gap between you and your little brother. Sarah lived in the house that used to be where yours is now. She and my aunt and uncle were from Scotland. Well, we're all from Scotland, but they'd only just come over. I loved to play with Sarah—when I was that young, I thought my teenage cousin with the fiery red hair was the best person in the world. I followed her everywhere.

One night, she snuck out and took my uncle's car. I raced to catch up so she would let me come too, but she didn't even see me. I waited in her yard until she came back. If I couldn't go with her, then I wanted to hear the story of her secret adventures.

"But I got tired and drifted off. It was a warm summer night, so I was comfortable. I don't know what time Sarah got home, but the approaching car woke me up. I saw it coming up the road, and as soon as it was in sight, off went the headlights. She didn't want to wake my aunt and uncle.

"I tell you that part, because without those headlights on, I could see right through the front windshield. I could see Sarah's face. We locked eyes as she pulled into the driveway, and at first she looked so delighted to spot me. She was always laughing when I got into trouble. But then she looked above me and her face got real scared. She jumped out of the car and shouted for me, telling me to run for her as fast as I could. Ooh I've never been so scared. Whatever she'd seen, I didn't want to look at. I ran straight into my cousin's arms."

"What did she see?" I asked.

"The Boogeyman," Landon said. "Standing behind Mom, waiting."

Mrs. Foster furled her eyebrow at Landon stealing her thunder. "That's what our parents told us, yes. That Sarah must have seen the Boogeyman. And she did. But those aren't the words she said that night. As she pulled me by the hand into her house and I asked her what was wrong, what did she see, she only repeated, 'teeth.'"

The hairs on my arms stood up. I knew those teeth, rotten and perfectly straight, and then more teeth stabbing through its skin, forming an irregular ring around its gray mouth. "That's what I saw."

She nodded. "Consider yourself fortunate, then."

"What? That thing is stalking my brother. It had picked him up last night. If I hadn't interrupted it, I don't know what it would have done. Dragged him back to that place it came from or used those rotten teeth on him right there." I could feel my emotions rising. "It's come two nights in a row. It'll come tonight. I don't know what to do."

Mrs. Foster let compassion show in her smile.

"Breathe, please. Your lack of sleep is making you only see the negative."

"What could the positive possibly be? You were almost taken by a monster and now it's after my little brother. And what did the Boogeyman have to do with the old house burning down?"

Mrs. Foster looked confused. "Not a thing. It was an electrical fire. Mice chewing on the wiring. Did Landon tell you the Boogeyman did that?"

"No," said Landon.

Hadn't he? I couldn't remember exactly what he'd said about it.

"Listen carefully," Mrs. Foster said. "I don't know whether the Boogeyman was born of fairy boggarts, or if he popped into existence after a million moms and dads told his story, but his only purpose is to scare children into staying safe. The real threat sixty years ago was a little girl sitting outside by herself at night, and a teenager sneaking off without her parents knowing where she was. You'd right believe Sarah never snuck out again, and I never spent another night outside alone. The Boogeyman keeps children in bed, where they're safe."

I didn't buy that for a second. "You're telling me that thing that was snatching my little brother from his crib—it wants to protect him?"

She tilted her head. "From what I hear, little Bennet would benefit from being scared to wander off."

There it was again—the guilt and blame about my

mistake of leaving the door open. "Bennet only went to the mailbox."

"Because that's where I found him," Landon said. "If I hadn't been there, who knows what would have happened?"

"What's done is done," Mrs. Foster said. "Don't scare her."

Landon interjected. "She needs to be afraid, and so does her brother. That's why the boogeyman is over there."

His mother conceded the point. "He's right. Once your brother is afraid enough, the Boogeyman will move on."

"You didn't hear him crying last night. I've never heard him so scared. Why isn't that enough?"

"I can't tell you the inner workings of the Boogeyman's heart."

"He wasn't scared enough yet," Landon said.

"What do I do if it comes again tonight?" I asked, already knowing their answer.

"Stay in your bed," Mrs. Foster said. "Be afraid and let your brother be afraid."

"He's not even two. I'm not leaving him alone with that thing."

"Part of being a parent—and I suppose an older sister —is doing for children what they need in the long run and not what they think they need right now."

I was getting tired of hearing that.

"I can't tell you what to do; you're not my child. But if you want the Boogeyman to move on, you let your brother endure this hard thing. It's what he needs."

I could feel my impulsivity mixing with anger. I didn't want to explode at my neighbors. "I have to go."

Landon and his mom gave me a grave goodbye.

As I walked out, I heard the beginning of a harsh lecture. "You tell me every detail about the situation in which you allowed your friend to use our patio to disobey her parents."

11

————

THE REST of the day went by too quickly.

I painted a watercolor rose. I watched a couple episodes of a Star Wars show. I tried to stay out in the living room, away from where I'd seen the Boogeyman.

My mind did circles around my conversation with Landon and his mom.

I don't know what I'd expected from them—clues to the Boogeyman's weakness or to learn that the reason behind Mrs. Foster's reservedness was that she was a secret monster hunter. But I didn't expect this bullshit about the Boogeyman being good for my little brother.

I'd heard his cries. Nothing good was coming from that fear. And I'd seen the Boogeyman. It had looked right at me. It felt vindictive.

Mrs. Foster certainly seemed to believe her story about the Boogeyman existing to protect children, but that was opposite of the aura I felt when it was standing over my little brother's crib.

But could I trust my gut feelings?

Ever since I turned sixteen, my exhaustion had me quicker to get angry, quicker to feel hopeless, and slower to recognize anything good. Was it possible the Boogeyman really was there to keep Bennet safe? If that were the case, was I even in a state where I could recognize that? Or would my tired brain only see the situation as negatively as possible?

If letting Bennet cry tonight would make the Boogeyman leave him alone, then that's what I should do.

But I couldn't talk myself into believing the thing I'd seen last night didn't mean my brother harm. I wanted it to be true, because then this could all be over. But wanting and believing were two different things.

I made a decision.

After Mom and Dad turned off their light, I'd go into Bennet's room. I'd hide in the closet and I'd watch through the slats in the door. If the Boogeyman arrived, I'd stay put. I'd let Bennet cry. But if the Boogeyman reached its disturbingly normal hands toward my little brother, then I'd be there to stop it.

I CONSIDERED ASKING my parents for permission to nap.

I even had a good excuse worked out—I wanted to go

for a hike the next day, and after missing sleep the last two nights, I really needed a few extra hours.

But I imagined calling Dad and asking for permission, only to hear the disappointment in his voice, and so I stayed awake the rest of the day.

After everyone was home and Bennet was in bed, I found my eyelids growing heavy.

When the lights went out, I snuck into Bennet's room. His white noise machine hummed.

I didn't hear his snoring.

Panic flashed inside me that the Boogeyman had already come and left. I went to his crib, straining to see in the dark. I risked using the glow of my phone's screen.

Bennet was sleeping facedown, his knees tucked up under him. His cheek rose and fell as air moved through his open lips. He'd chosen to sleep with the board book version of *The Little Blue Truck*.

He was still here.

And I would make sure it stayed that way.

I checked under the crib, to once again see only the two plastic tubs that should have been there.

The room was safe for now.

But it was too dark. There was a piece of electrical tape covering up the ON/OFF button on the white noise machine. I removed it, letting an LED shine bright. Its only purpose was to make it possible to find the button in the dark, but its bright white light "hurt sleeping conditions" and so Dad had covered it up.

That would be enough light for me to see if the Boogeyman came into the room.

I carefully slid open the closet door and then closed it behind me.

I lowered myself into a sitting position and checked that I could see between the slats. It was a very limited view, but I could see Bennet's crib and the space beside it.

I squeezed my fingers around a steak knife that I'd borrowed from the kitchen. If the Boogeyman tried to touch Bennet, then I'd be able to do more than scare it. And if I couldn't stay awake, I could prick my own fingers.

I tried to remain uncomfortable as I settled in for the night.

12

IT COULD HAVE BEEN 10 minutes, an hour, or three.

Time moved funny in that closet, peering between closet door slats into a room lit by the LED ON/OFF button of a white noise machine.

My chin drooped, only for me to catch myself, bounce my head back up, and then repeat it all again. When I gained enough clarity of mind to realize what was happening, I'd poke the tip of my thumb with the steak knife. Not enough to draw blood, but enough to hurt.

I'd missed too much sleep the past two nights. My mind was going absolutely loopy.

I stood up to stay awake, only to find myself sitting down again.

At one point, I knew with a certainty that the Boogeyman was crawling out from under Bennet's crib. But I stared and waited and nothing came into view.

After that length of time that could have been 10

minutes, an hour, or three, I caught myself nodding off again.

I pricked my thumb with the knife, too hard.

Blood dripped down my hand.

It pooled in the lines of my palm, catching the LED light which shone in sheets between the closet door slats. Bright red against the dark.

The skinny pools overflowed. Blood ran down my wrist, my elbow, to the floor.

How was there so much? Why was it so cold on my arm?

I had to move my legs or my pajama pants would get stained.

The pool of blood on the carpet grew larger, deeper, until I was backed up into the corner of Bennet's closet.

My blood formed a rectangle, covering the closet floor in its entirety. The hanging toddler clothes and stack of cardboard boxes remained dusky shapes in the darkness, but my blood reflected as much light as it would outside at noon.

And then I saw this pool of my blood extend through the back corner of the closet. It was like watching water run down the ditch in a heavy rainstorm, except it was my blood spreading to fill out a narrow hallway that appeared off the back of Bennet's closet.

I was so dumb. Not only for cutting my thumb and making a mess, but for assuming that the only pathway into the Boogeyman's lair was under the crib. Hadn't I ever heard a scary story before? Of course the Boogeyman could come through the closet.

I walked through my blood. It was cold and sticky against my bare feet. It touched the bottom of my pajama pants and weighed them down like I'd fallen in a swimming pool.

My back to the closet door, I looked down this new hallway.

The Boogeyman stood twenty feet away, silhouetted by a yellow glow from farther down the hallway.

In the monster's black silhouette I saw its gray and rotting teeth—not the perfectly straight teeth inside its mouth, but the ring of horizontal teeth that pierced through skin. Like my blood that ran past my feet to fill the hall floor, the Boogeyman's teeth stood out in the darkness, perfectly visible, perfectly bright. Perfectly rotten.

That oblong ring of teeth lifted on either edge. It was smiling at me. The Boogeyman went down to its knees, thick, stiff arms bending in a gentle curve. Then it brought its overstuffed arms and small hands to the floor. It lay its face into my blood, prostrating itself before me.

I thought it might worship me, that this was what I needed although I didn't understand why.

And then the slurping began.

It sucked my lifeblood into its mouth, through its lips, through each protruding tooth.

Inside my body, I felt my blood vacuumed through my veins and toward the wound in my thumb. My blood didn't want to leave and so it held onto my veins so tightly that my arms and my legs and my ears felt sucked inward.

This was what I needed.

Not losing my blood. That part was bad and would only keep hurting.

But the Boogeyman had a purpose and once the last drop of blood fell from my thumb, I would finally deserve all the good he'd done for me.

My head grew light.

My vision blurred, except for the glow of my blood, except for those pinpoints of rotten teeth.

The Boogeyman's head shot up, faded eyes now leering at me compassionately.

I knew those eyes.

I'd felt that love and that condemnation.

I snapped awake.

I was sitting on the closet floor. My thumb was not bleeding. There was no hallway in the back of the closet.

Bennet was crying, but he wasn't in his room. His cries were too far away.

As I stiffly climbed to my feet, I prayed that Mom or Dad had come and brought him to their room.

I pushed on the door. It didn't open.

Bennet's bookshelf had been pushed in front of the closet.

13

I SCREAMED FOR DAD. I rattled the closet door. I threw myself at it. Board books fell from the shelf that locked me in here.

Bennet's cries diminished as he was carried further away.

I yelled for Mom.

Their lamps clicked on, their bedroom door opened—I could tell because the white LED from Bennet's white noise machine was joined by the yellow incandescent light from down the hallway.

Heavy, overlapping footsteps as Mom and Dad came running.

"Rachel?" Dad's voice was angry but with a touch of concern. He assumed I was imagining things again, but he could hear my fear.

"Get Bennet!" I cried.

Through the slats in the closet door, I watched Dad run into the dark room and lean down into Bennet's crib.

"Where is he?" Dad was still angry. "Do you have him?" He looked around the room for me.

"It took him!" I yelled. "I told you it was real."

"Why are you in the closet? Do you have your brother?"

"No! That thing trapped me in here!" I wanted to scream at him, to tell him he was stupid for thinking that I'd somehow taken Bennet into the closet with me and then moved the bookshelf to trap us both inside. Except I also didn't want to do that because while the words might be stupid, the fact that Dad had said them meant that I needed to understand how they *weren't* stupid.

Dad pulled away the bookshelf to open the door. "Do you have Bennet?" he asked again.

"No!" I pushed past him into the room. I checked Bennet's crib myself, knowing he was already gone.

Mom came down the hallway. "What's going on? Where's Bennet?"

"That thing took him," I said. I got down on my belly to look under the crib. I only saw the two plastic tubs.

The way had already closed.

"Get off the floor. This isn't funny," Mom said. "Where's your brother?"

"She was in the closet when I came in here," Dad said. "The bookshelf was in front of the door."

Mom's breathing grew louder, more panicked. "Check in her room," she said to Dad.

Dad rushed back into the hallway. "Not here!"

I heard him run to check the living room.

He wouldn't be there. The Boogeyman had already taken him and it was my fault. I'd fallen asleep.

Or had the Boogeyman taken him because I didn't stay in my room like Mrs. Foster told me to? Because I hadn't trusted that the Boogeyman was only there to instill healthy fear?

Was Bennet gone forever? Or would the Boogeyman return my little brother once he'd learned to be afraid— was this a supernatural version of one of those "scared-straight" camps?

I stayed on my knees next to Bennet's crib. What else could I do?

Mom stood over me. "Where is he?"

She was panicking. I knew the hate that emanated from her wasn't intentional. It was fear for Bennet.

"It took him under the crib."

Mom bent down to look for herself. She pulled out the two plastic storage tubs. "There's nothing under here."

This wasn't my fault. This was Landon and his mom's fault for convincing me that the Boogeyman didn't mean any real harm. If I hadn't been in that closet... I might have slept through the kidnapping anyways.

Mom grabbed me by the chin. "Where is your brother?"

"It took him. I was going to stop it if it came, but I fell asleep. I'm so sorry." That's why it happened, why my brother was gone: because I was too weak to stay awake.

I'd finally done it. I'd destroyed my family with my weakness.

Mom looked at me with fear. I understood why. Or I thought I did. Looking back now, it wasn't that she thought I was weak but that she worried I'd lost my mind and done something to Bennet.

But then Dad came back in the room, on the phone with the police. "Yes, we've looked everywhere. He can't climb out of his crib. I don't know, I'll check." He went to the windows. "The doors are locked. The windows are locked. I don't understand."

The tight anger in my Mom's cheeks drooped slightly, betraying her fear. "What are you doing? He's got to be here somewhere."

She followed Dad out of the room.

I was left on the floor next to the crib.

"Please," I whispered. "Bring him back. I'm sorry. Give me another chance and I'll stay awake. I'm strong enough —I know I am."

I lay forward on my knees, prostrated like the Boogeyman in my dream. The soft rug caressed my cheek. Beneath the crib there was nothing but dust. The tunnel I'd seen before was gone.

I didn't want to keep staring at the spot where I'd lost my brother and so I turned my head the opposite way, laying my other cheek on the rug.

Bennet's bedroom light was still off. Mom and Dad had searched for him by the light of their own bedroom lamps, the yellow light coming in through the hallway.

From my view down here on the floor, Bennet's open doorway loomed over me. It glowed a yellow rectangle.

My breath caught and I sat up.

Disparate thoughts clicked together and I kicked myself for not seeing it earlier.

I reached under Bennet's crib, not knowing exactly what I was looking for, only that it would be reflective.

The rug ended right at the edge of the crib. Beyond that was the hardwood floor which Dad meticulously cleaned and polished.

I scratched my fingernails along the flooring until they caught on something. I pulled and a section of boards bounced. They briefly reflected the light from the hallway.

I found the indent again and this time I wedged my fingernail in firmly. I pulled.

A long section of the wood rotated up as if on a hinge. It fit just right to block my view of under the crib.

Dad's skill with floor polishing had been more than effective. In the dark, with the light behind me, the floorboards worked as a blurry mirror.

There was the chair, there was the bookshelf, and there was the yellow glowing doorway that had been haunting my thoughts since I saw this reflection two nights ago.

There was no otherworldly Boogeyman's lair.

No crooked room.

Only a reflection of Bennet's own bedroom.

There was no glowing yellow doorway.

Only Bennet's own doorway lit by my parents' bedside lamps.

My dreams had been terrorized by a reflection.

A reflection off shiny floorboards that lifted up underneath my brother's crib, blocking the view behind them.

They were hiding something.

I jumped to my feet to wrestle the heavy crib out of my way. I needed to see what was behind the shiny raised floorboards. It was heavier than I'd expected, but I managed to rotate it away from the wall.

Underneath, the lifted floorboards revealed a long rectangle of cement foundation, and in the middle: a hole.

The hole was oblong. Less than two feet long and one foot wide. Its cement edges were marred with chips and grooves. The cement went down about a foot, and then there was only blackness.

With the only light in the room still the white LED and the long reaching yellow light from down the hall, I couldn't see where the hole led.

But I could see one thing about it:

It was real.

There was nothing confusing to it, not like when I'd thought the reflection of Bennet's room was an otherworldly realm. Or like how the Boogeyman's extra teeth pierced through his skin and his eyes seemed to only half-exist. (Those eyes, something about those eyes that my dream had reminded me, how they loved what I could be, how they despised what I was.)

This hole in front of me was *real*.

And down there was where the Boogeyman had taken my brother.

14

_____

My mind swirled around the Boogeyman.

Those lifted floorboards that had blocked my view of the hole and reflected Bennet's room—were those an intentional misdirect? Why would an ancient evil—or an ancient protective monster—hide how it was entering a room?

I'd misunderstood the reflection that I'd seen—was I misunderstanding what I saw about the Boogeyman itself?

Why did its eyes look familiar, even as they blurred with its skin, only half existing?

A thousand questions swirled through my head but they were only distractions. I didn't want to think about them.

I'd found the path to go after Bennet.

My eyes locked on the dark hole in the cement foundation. I yelled for Mom and Dad.

Mom came rushing in. "Is he in here?" She saw the hole in the floor. "What is that?"

"That's where it took Bennet."

Realization washed over her expression. Her eyes widened with fear and regret. "There was really someone here?"

I nodded.

"How did anyone fit down there?" Mom got on her knees to look down the hole. "Bennet!"

She motioned to me. "We need a flashlight. Get your father. He went outside to wait for the police."

The longer we waited to chase the Boogeyman down that hole, the farther away it could get. The more time it'd have to complete its intentions for my little brother. But I decided it'd be faster to run to the front door and back than to argue with Mom.

I ran out onto our front porch, but when I looked around outside I didn't see Dad, just the dark neighborhood. "Dad?" In response, I heard only the call of crickets and chirper frogs.

I ran back inside.

Mom was down the hole to her hips, but she wasn't going any deeper. The opening was too narrow.

"My baby's down there," she wailed, wriggling herself tighter.

"Get back out before you get stuck."

"I can't leave him."

"You don't fit! Get out and let me down." I had to go after

Bennet. Not because I was the only one who would fit, but because it was my fault he was taken. If I hadn't fallen asleep, if I'd done better at convincing Mom and Dad, if I was strong enough to not be so tired that I thought I was delusional.

I helped Mom shimmy back out from the hole in the floor.

"Is your dad coming?"

"I couldn't find him," I said, not wanting to waste anymore time.

"Wait here," she said. "I'll go get him."

"I'm going after Bennet," I said.

"It's not safe. Wait while I find your father." Mom left.

I waited until I heard the front door open and then I lowered myself down.

My feet and knees fit through but the edges of the cement slab foundation scraped against my thighs. I should have changed into jeans. My pajama pants did little to shield me from the rough edges.

I lifted myself onto my hands and dipped lower. My feet dangled in emptiness under the floor. I squeezed my stomach and chest through. I had to turn my head to fit through the oblong hole. For a moment when the cement was against my cheek, I thought I would suddenly develop claustrophobia.

And then my head was through and I was dangling in the dark.

I kicked around, feeling for anything to step on.

My foot collided with something which toppled with a

clatter. That sound wasn't far below me. It'd be safe to drop.

I let go and fell.

MY FEET LANDED on a divot in the ground. I went limp to avoid twisting my ankle and ended up on my butt in soft dirt.

My eyes adjusted to the dark.

The hole above me let down enough light to see, just barely.

On the dirt floor was a pile of cement pieces, directly below where the hole had been scratched upwards into the cement. Next to me was a wooden ladder on its side. That's what I'd kicked over.

It struck me as weird that a supernatural monster created by centuries of parents' protective impulses would need a wooden step ladder to get up to the ceiling.

Earlier I couldn't get its teeth out of my mind. Mrs. Foster said her cousin had seen the Boogeyman and said the same thing: *teeth*.

But now what plagued me were its eyes. Despite only being half-there, they seemed so normal.

I turned on my phone's flashlight.

That house that used to be here was so big, Landon had said. It had three stories and a basement.

I'd found the basement.

"Bennet?" I called.

It was a square room, about as big as our house. The walls were old stone and mortar, although they'd collapsed in at least two place, letting clay dirt spill through.

Stone and mortar pillars held up boards that went across the ceiling, which was made of rotten wood and dirt. In some places, that organic material had been scraped aside to reveal our home's cement foundation.

I crept around the pillars, searching all the dark corners of this damp space.

In one spot there was a particularly large pile of cement chunks. I shined my light upward. Another hole through our foundation. It ended at the floorboards above. If those boards were loose like the ones in Bennet's room, I couldn't tell.

I wasn't sure *where* this second hole was. It was closer to the side of the house, so probably under Mom and Dad's room.

A supernatural entity definitely wouldn't have dug upward under the wrong room.

And so I wasn't surprised at what I found when I inspected the side wall of the basement, hidden behind a pillar.

A patch of stone and mortar had collapsed.

Someone had dug a tunnel through the dirt behind it.

Short, dark, and held up by posts and boards, I'd have to crawl to fit through it.

But obviously I would, because that tunnel aimed straight for Landon's house.

BEFORE I COULD HIT my knees, Mom called to me from above. "I told you not to go down there!"

I ran underneath the hole. "There's a tunnel going to the Fosters' house!"

I heard her talking to herself. "The police are almost here. I'm going next door with your father. You climb back up and wait for the police."

I wasn't waiting for anybody. Mom and Dad knew where Bennet was now, so I could leave it to them. But I was closest and it was my fault and so I was going after him.

I ran back to the dark tunnel and practically dove inside. The dirt was cold this far beneath the surface of the earth.

I bumped one of the posts. The board it was holding up fell. Dirt rained down. My heart leapt, anticipating the eight feet of earth that were about to collapse upon me. But then the rain stopped.

I pushed forward into the darkness, my phone's light flashing wildly as I crawled.

My slow pace gave time for my exhausted mind to examine what was going on.

Those eyes...

Not those *teeth* that stuck out through skin, that Mrs. Foster's cousin had seen and that had scared her straight.

But those eyes.

Only half there. Faded. Blended with the gray skin around them.

I knew those eyes.

I didn't know why he would take Bennet, but I knew that he did.

A faint scent of too-ripe watermelon wafted into my nostrils, joining the damp smell of dirt.

For all my surety of what I was about to find, I couldn't explain the overly sweet fragrance that had accompanied the strangeness I'd experienced the last two nights.

Electric light shone ahead.

I'd nearly reached the end of the tunnel.

I turned off my own light to hide my approach. As I got close, the space outside the tunnel came into view.

It was the storage room off to the side of the Fosters' basement. A bare lightbulb hung from the ceiling. A stack of bricks filled one corner. A pile of dirt filled another, the byproduct of the tunnel excavation.

A wooden door separated this storage room from the rest of the basement. It was closed.

In front of it crouched the Boogeyman, holding my little brother.

15

THERE WAS the Boogeyman in its dingy yellow raincoat, just as tall as I remembered, but now the thick arms and legs looked more like oversized clothes than bulky limbs.

It faced the door to the rest of the basement, its back to me.

Over its shoulder I could see the top of Bennet's head, his thin blond hair visible while he buried his face in the Boogeyman's shoulder, hiding from the monster that held him.

Before I could crawl out from the tunnel, the Boogeyman let out a panicked warning. "Stay back."

I froze.

But it wasn't talking to me. I'd intruded on a conversation already going on through that old wooden door.

I climbed out from the tunnel and said the Boogeyman's name. "Landon."

He turned around.

Now that this costume stood under the direct glow of even a single lightbulb, its slipshod quality was evident.

The Boogeyman didn't have strangely thick arms and legs. Landon had stuffed the arms of the raincoat and the legs of his pants.

The mask fit Landon's head well. The neck was tucked under the collar of his shirt. The dark, stringy hair looked real enough, but the gray rubber skin looked fake. The teeth which stuck through the rubber skin were a higher quality than the rest of the mask—Landon must have added those himself.

Black mesh covered the mask's eye holes.

Landon's panicked brown eyes were visible through the mesh, but only partly.

In my half-delusional exhaustion, I'd seen his eyes as half-existing.

"Stay back," he said again, this time to me. He turned Bennet away from me.

"It's okay," I told my brother. "I'm here."

"Tico?" Bennet tried to look at me but Landon held my brother's head tight against his shoulder.

Landon's skinny hands sticking out from those stuffed sleeves looked ridiculous. But he was still a mostly-grown teenager and Bennet was a toddler.

"Give me my brother," I ordered calmly as I approached.

"I said stay back!" Landon took another step away from me. He raised Bennet above his head, threatening to dash him against the stack of bricks.

My heart dropped to my stomach. I stopped dead, giving Landon space. "Don't hurt him. Why would you hurt him?"

Bennet started to cry.

Pounding on the door.

Dad's voice. "Let us in!" I'd never heard him so scared.

Mrs. Foster spoke. "Landon? This isn't how it works. Please open the door."

And then a threat from Mom, "You should end this before the police get here."

I inched closer, ready to dive for Bennet if Landon threw him down.

"What are you doing?" I pleaded. "Aren't we friends?"

Behind the mask's eye mesh, I saw doubt.

"You haven't been listening," Landon said.

I frantically tried to think of when he'd opened up to me and I'd ignored him. But if there was a day we didn't talk in person, then we texted.

A loud impact against the door. Dad trying to kick it open.

Landon yelled, raspy. "Stop or you won't see your son again."

While he was facing the door I inched closer.

Mrs. Foster's voice came through. "Please honey, you don't understand what you're doing. This isn't how it works."

"They're not afraid enough," Landon said.

"Why do you want me afraid?" I asked.

"Rachel?" Mom had heard me. "If you're in there, open this door."

"Don't do anything dangerous," Dad yelled. "Stay calm."

Neither of them were in here with me. If I screwed up, it wasn't them who'd have to watch Bennet get dashed against a brick's sharp corner.

"Please let me hold him," I begged.

"No!" Landon snapped. "Stop trying to interfere! If you'd just done what you were told, none of this would have been necessary."

I was trying very hard to stay calm, but it's difficult not to let rage overtake you when you haven't slept much in six months and your crazy neighbor is threatening your little brother's life.

"Necessary? You wanted me to sit and watch the Boogeyman scare Bennet! That's not necessary—that's insane!"

"Please be calm," Dad begged through the door. "We'll let the police fix this."

"Bennet needed to be scared!" Landon argued. "He might get hurt if he wandered outside alone again. We told you that."

I heard arguing between the adults on the far side of the door. Probably Mom demanding to know how involved Mrs. Foster was with this kidnapping.

"So you dressed up as the Boogeyman? Did your mom make up that story about her cousin?"

"No," Landon said. "That's real. It's all real. But we don't decide when the Boogeyman helps, and so I had to step up."

"No you didn't," called his mom.

"This is what's necessary," Landon yelled back.

"How does stealing my brother in the night help him?"

Landon's arms quivered at the effort of holding Bennet above his head. "This isn't about him anymore. He's plenty scared now. This is about you. You're not scared enough."

"Me? Scared enough of what?"

"You're not listening to your parents. You used me to get around their rules. I thought you regretted it, but just yesterday you casually confessed to my mom like disobeying your parents had been a minor thing."

"What are you talking about?"

"You slept at my house. You guilted me into letting you and then you told on me."

Landon was a teenager afraid of being tattled on. How could I possibly reason with him?

"I didn't mean to get you in trouble. I'm not going to nap anymore. I promise."

"Why should I believe that? Every time we talk you complain about how tired you are. You're not really trying to obey your parents. You're still arguing with them in your head. That's not safe. You have to learn to be scared. To be safe."

He was serious. I wanted to leap forward to grab my brother, but Landon was a foot taller than me. I wasn't strong enough to safely wrestle Bennet away, and that had nothing to do with self-perception—only body mass.

"Okay. Fine. I'm scared. I won't complain about the sleep schedule anymore. Please just give me Bennet."

"You're lying." Landon jerked him away from me, prompting a shriek within Bennet's sobs.

"Be gentle with him!" I breathed deep, trying to find some calm like Dad had told me to do. "This makes no sense. What do you want me to say? I'm already doing my best to do what my parents tell me. It's hard. It hurts. And I feel like shit every day because I can't do it. But apparently, you've looked into my soul and seen that I have doubts that this is the best way to live?"

Landon took off the mask. It must have been hot under there, because sweat beaded on his cheeks.

He had a bruise under his left eye, which hadn't been there yesterday. Before I'd inadvertently told on him to his mother.

Landon caught me looking at the bruise. "It's fine. It's what I needed."

My response was a swirl of emotions that I couldn't articulate. So I said, "No."

He lowered Bennet to his side. "I know you. You'll be happier when you obey your parents. I know I am. That's why I had to scare you."

Mrs. Foster banged on the door. "That's not how it works. He doesn't want you acting for him."

Landon kept his compassionate, disdainful eyes locked on me while he answered his mother. "You said everyone needed to listen to their parents. Otherwise the Boogeyman would come."

"Yes, the Boogeyman. Not you."

"I'm helping," Landon whispered. "I'm helping Rachel."

"Why do you care?" I demanded.

He scoffed and then offered me a smile. "Because I love you."

I was taken aback. This was because he had a crush on me? When had his mind twisted so much?

"I'm helping you," Landon said. "This is what you need."

Something snapped inside me. "You don't get to tell me what I need."

Landon looked indignant. "You don't even know what's going on. You didn't know about the Boogeyman until this week. But you'll understand as you learn more. You just have to trust me right now."

Three hard knocks on the door. A stranger's voice. The police were here.

"I'll never trust you again. You're hurting me. This isn't better for me in the long run. This isn't learning not to touch a hot stove." I felt six months of anger spill out. My rant thickly filled the air, joining the scent of too-sweet melon. "You think I'm ever gonna be able to sleep again after you threatened to throw my little brother against those bricks? You see me as some dream girl who only needs to learn *one little thing* and you take it upon yourself to fix that? I'm fine the way I am. Leave me alone."

Landon glared at me with fury.

I'd made it worse.

He raised Bennet back above his head, above the edges and corners of the bricks.

I gagged at the scent of sweet, rotting fruit.

Without fanfare, the Boogeyman suddenly stood beside Landon.

Landon's costume had it all wrong, but oh, cousin Sarah had it right about one thing: *teeth*.

I thought I'd felt fear before.

I hadn't.

Bennet wailed.

My impulsivity overcame my fear and I jumped forward to snatch my brother away from my insane neighbor.

Landon looked the Boogeyman in the face, his eyes only coming level to the monster's mouth. His arms went limp just as I reached them.

I caught my little brother.

"Tico!" Bennet cried, scared and relieved and full of confusing and overwhelming emotion that I thought only toddlers could feel, except being in this basement room with that *thing* was flaring a new level of terror through my body and mind.

I held Bennet to my chest and ran for the door. I fumbled with the latch, keeping my head down, not wanting to see those teeth (*teeth*) again.

I waited for Landon to scream but I only heard the rustle of his raincoat.

I gathered my courage to look behind me.

I saw Landon's feet dragged into the tunnel, into the old basement he'd used to trick me.

And then he did scream, loud and terrified and echoing far more than was possible in that little tunnel, in that basement. His scream echoed like he was somewhere cold and cavernous.

I got the latch open.

Two cops stood there, ready to kick it down. Mom pushed past them to pull me and Bennet close to her. Dad wrapped us all in his arms.

Mrs. Foster followed the cops through the door, but they didn't find Landon.

No one ever did.

16
___

AFTER THEY CLEARED THE HOUSE, the cops let us go home. We walked through our dark yards while flashing lights cruised through the neighborhood.

We all four sat on the couch. Bennet sat in Mom's lap but with his head on my shoulder.

One cop was posted at our front porch, another at our back door. We could hear them moving around in the basement beneath us.

A knock.

Mom maneuvered Bennet fully onto me and then opened the front door. I heard Mrs. Foster ask if she could search our house for Landon.

Dad got up and shut the door before Mom could answer. "The cops already searched. It's not that big of a house."

Mom checked on Bennet and then went to the garage. She came back with a hammer, nails, and plywood.

There was banging from Bennet's room.

A minute later Mom rejoined us on the couch.

After some time, Dad broke the silence. "I was so scared."

Nobody had to say that we were, too. I didn't tell them about the real Boogeyman.

"I'm sorry I didn't believe you," Mom said.

I didn't say anything. That's not the apology I wanted.

The police never found Landon. Their best guess was that he'd fled into the old basement, up through our house, and then he'd cut town.

Dad took off work for the rest of the summer since he didn't like me or Bennet being out of his sight for long.

Mom had a backhoe come out and then a dump truck full of gravel. Dad said we should have an engineer make sure the foundation was secure, but Mom insisted on filling in the old basement.

I frequently woke up from nightmares and went to check on Bennet. I'd find him sleeping peacefully. Often, I'd find either Mom or Dad asleep in the nursery rocking chair.

Despite my bad dreams and being too scared to get up and go pee in the middle of the night, I never did smell too-sweet watermelon in our house again.

Mrs. Foster went completely reclusive. She moved away shortly before I left for college.

Leaving for school was bittersweet. Bennet was nearly four and already reading—or at least memorizing his favorite books. It hurt to only see him when I visited. But it was time for me to move out. See, although I loved and I still love Mom and Dad, in my last two years of living at home they got tired of arguing with me all the time.

They said I slept too much.

READ THIS NEXT

Hello Strange Reader,

Stephen King has Constant Readers. But you just read a book about the monster under the bed. I figure you'll proudly wear the mantle of "Strange Reader."

And so, Strange Reader, *thank you* for reading.

Please take a few seconds to rate it or even write out a review. I read them all, and I appreciate the good and the bad. They help my weird little books find more homes.

If you want to stay up to date with my new releases, plus hear my book recommendations for Strange Readers like you and me, you can sign up for my email newsletter at BenFarthing.com.

If you'd like to order a signed copy of this or other books, or grab stickers, fridge magnets, or other merch, go to my etsy store: TheDreadFarthing.

You've now seen my style of weird horror in creepy

places, with plots driven by the urge to discover *what the hell is happening?*

From here, I recommend *Those Who Dwell Below the Sidewalk.* Here's what it's about:

Beneath the city, they are watching...

During a bumper-to-bumper commute, Everard is almost murdered by a woman whose skin is covered in a living swarm of holes. Furious, Everard chases her down an impossible staircase. He's thrown into the city's supernatural underbelly where nightmares lurk around every corner.

In this world within the city's periphery, strange cults protect their members from monsters of urban legends. But something is riling up those monsters. Something ancient and evil, which has set its hungry sights on Everard.

For fans of horror epics like Stephen King's *Dark Tower* or the wondrous horrors of Clive Barker's *Cabal* & *Nightbreed*, Ben Farthing's *The Who Dwell Below the Sidewalk* is "non-stop terrifying action" with a villain who *Apex Magazine* Editor Lesley Conner called, "The stuff of my freaking nightmares."

Those Who Dwell Below the Sidewalk is available as an ebook, paperback, and audiobook.

Keep reading for a look at my other books.

IT WAITS ON THE TOP FLOOR

The tower appeared overnight, but it wants to keep you forever.

"If you like dark, twisted, raise-the-hair-on-the-back-of-your-neck horror, you can't go wrong with this book!" - Booknerdia

Thursday night, it was a dirt lot.

Friday morning, it was a 60-story skyscraper.

A tech billionaire wants the building's secrets for herself. She hires a team to reverse-engineer the overnight construction. But she knows more than she's letting on.

A curious 9-year-old decides there's treasure inside, and goes exploring. His terrified dad chases close behind. Inside, the facade of an empty office building is quickly shattered. Ghostly figures stalk the explorers. The walls themselves are hungry. And something is waiting on the top floor.

It Waits On the Top Floor is the first book in the *Horror Lurks Beneath* trilogy. It's available as an ebook, paperback, and audiobook.

THE PIPER'S GRAVEYARD

A mysterious evil haunts a small town's radio waves.

★ ★ ★ ★ ★ *"A scary atmosphere and great characters."* *Goodreads Review.*

Cessy returns home to search for her missing sister.

She finds a half-abandoned town under siege by unexplainable threats: Attics and crawlspaces stretch into endless tunnels. Corpses turn up riddled with holes— holes that slither through flesh like insectile parasites. It all leads deep into the abandoned coal mine.

Cessy's sister disappeared while investigating the vengeful voice on the radio. To find her, Cessy will have to unravel the dark mystery wriggling up from the coal mine.

The Piper's Graveyard is available as an ebook, paperback, and audiobook.

CROWDED CHASMS: TALES IN TERRIFYING PLACES

Short Stories Set in Weird and Scary Places

Lost in an endless forest, a spelling-bee champ follows the powerlines far above. But where do they lead?

In the steam tunnels under the school, a student finds a bone tied in a knot. He should have left it there.

After their minivan swerves off a cliff, a family wakes up in an empty Heaven.

Two spelunkers release an ancient evil. Their only hope is to find order in the demon's chaos.

In this collection of Weird Horror stories, Ben Farthing delivers his unique brand of surreal horror and strange happenings.

Crowded Chasms is currently available as an ebook. Paperback and audiobook are in production.

ABOUT THE AUTHOR

Ben Farthing writes supernatural horror. He lives with his wife and children near Richmond, Virginia. Follow him on Facebook, Instagram, and TikTok.

9 798330 410798